How Got Their Colours

• Tales from the Australian Dreamtime •

Written by Helen Chapman

Illustrated by Fay Martin

Contents

Collins

How the birds got their colours

Back in the Dreamtime, when the land and animals
were being made, all the birds were the same
colour – black! It didn't matter if the bird was big
like Cassowary or small like Budgerigar, fluffy like
Kookaburra or smooth like Brolga – they all had
black feathers. But this was about to change.

One day, Dove was flying far away from home. He was
looking for food to share with his friends, when he
saw some tasty-looking grubs crawling on the ground.
Dove swooped to catch them but, when he landed,
a sharp stick from a broken-off tree branch stabbed deep
into his foot. Dove fell over and as he lay there, his foot
began to burn and swell.

Poor Dove called for help, but none of his friends heard or saw him. For days, he lay alone and in pain, until finally he was discovered by the other birds.

They were shocked by what they saw. Dove's foot was red and swollen and he'd become very ill. The kind birds fluttered around him to try and help. Some spread wide their wings to shade his body or flapped their wings to cool him. Others flew to a water hole and carried back water in their beaks. They trickled droplets into Dove's dry mouth and splashed water over his hot foot to soothe the pain.

But one bird did nothing: Crow! He was selfish and annoyed, and jealous of the attention that Dove was getting. Why should he bother wasting his time caring for such a sick bird? Nothing could save him. But the other birds didn't care what Crow thought, and after hours of listening to his grumbling, they chased him away.

Poor Dove's foot looked bad. It was getting hotter and more swollen all the time. Dove's good friends were upset. Helping him was all very well, but it wasn't making him better. They had to do more. Each bird thought about why Dove was such a good friend and each came up with a plan to help in their own special way.

Dove always cheered Kookaburra up on the mornings she didn't feel like laughing. So now Kookaburra perched by her friend and told her best joke. She hoped Dove would shake with laughter and the nasty stick would flick out of his foot. But the stick didn't move.

Dove used to skip and hop to teach Cassowary new
dance steps. So now Cassowary stood over his friend
and stomped the ground with his big feet. He hoped
the horrid stick would shake with the vibrations and
shoot right out of Dove's foot. But the stick didn't move.

Dove and Parrot liked to look for food together.
Sometimes they'd have to tug hard to pull out grubs,
which were stuck in the ground. This gave Parrot
an idea. She hopped over to Dove, and with her sharp,
hooked beak, she pulled the stick out from Dove's
swollen foot to let the swelling drain out.

And as she did so, the colours of birds as we know them today were created. All of nature's brilliant colours exploded from Dove's foot and flew over Parrot's black body. Bright rosy red splashed on to her beak, blue violet over her head and belly, bright green on to her wings, tail and back, and orange and yellow across her chest. Parrot dazzled like a rainbow in her new colours. This was her reward for being such a good and clever friend.

Colours also flew over all the other kind and thoughtful birds, to thank them for looking after Dove. Some like kind Budgerigar were splattered in a mixture of many colours, while others like helpful Brolga were sprayed with only a few. Some of the caring birds were decorated with stripes or spots. They all became beautifully coloured, including brave Dove. Apart from stripes of black across his wings and back, the darkness drained from Dove's feathers and they became pastel grey, brown and pink.

But one bird stayed black: Crow! Being selfish meant he'd been too far away from Dove to receive any of the wonderful new colours. And that's why Crow remains stuck with his plain black feathers to this day.

How the koala lost his tail

Back in the Dreamtime, Koala's tail was long and furry.
He loved nothing more than showing it off to his
friends and admiring it in the reflection of
the water hole. Koala was best friends with
Tree Kangaroo. When Koala wasn't
busy grooming and brushing his tail,
the friends ate, played and napped
in the trees together.

But then no rain came for a whole year. All the streams and water holes slowly dried up. Still, Koala and Tree Kangaroo weren't worried. Their water came from eating leaves and they could go for a long time without climbing down to find more water. Koala did miss not seeing his tail reflected in the water, but he discovered that if he bent over and peered between his legs, he could see the tip which was still quite magnificent.

One morning, when Koala bit into a leaf, it was so dry that it crunched into powder in his mouth. "We'll soon run out of food and water," he said to Tree Kangaroo.

Tree Kangaroo climbed across the tree to Koala. "When I lived in Mum's pouch, we had a drought like this," he said. "To find water, Mum jumped down and left our tree. She found a dry stream bed and dug. She dug for hours."

"Did she find water?" asked Koala, as he decorated his tail with gum blossom.

"A little bit," said Tree Kangaroo. "It was enough for us to have a good drink."

Koala was excited. "Let's try that," he said.

Tree Kangaroo leapt to the ground and Koala climbed down, being careful not to dirty his tail. When they found a stream bed, it was dusty and dry.

Koala whined. "I'm tired and thirsty. Why don't you start digging? I'll rest for a bit; then I'll dig while you rest."

Tree Kangaroo began to dig. It was hard work to find water. Lazy Koala fluffed up his beautiful tail, snuggled into it and fell soundly asleep.

Tree Kangaroo kept on digging. After a while, his paws began to hurt. He called out to Koala, "Wake up. It's your turn."

Koala began to climb down into the dry river bed. Suddenly he cried, "Eew! My tail's got tangled in a spider's web. I need to stop and clean it so it's beautiful again. Keep digging."

Tree Kangaroo kept digging. The hole got deeper, but still there was no water. Tree Kangaroo called out to Koala again, "I'm tired. It's your turn to dig."

Again, Koala began to climb down. Suddenly, he cried, "I feel dizzy. I'll fall if I move. Keep digging."

Tree Kangaroo kept digging. At last, some water slowly began to trickle and fill the hole. Tree Kangaroo yelled, excitedly, "Water! I found it!"

When Koala heard this, his tail waggled with happiness. He jumped down and rushed to the hole, pushing Tree Kangaroo out of his way. Koala stuck his head in the water and began to gulp. He was so thirsty!

Tree Kangaroo was hopping mad. "Slow down," he said. "Save some for me!"

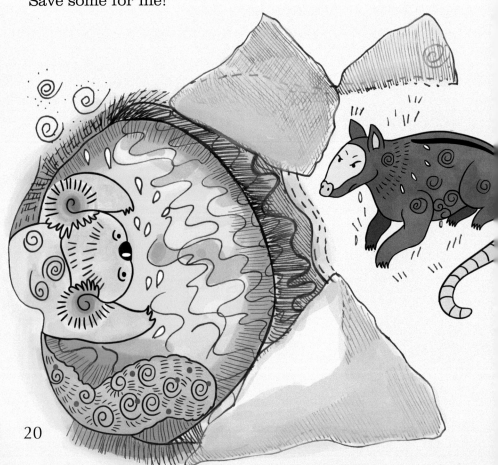

But Koala kept on
drinking and wouldn't stop. Tree Kangaroo grabbed
Koala's long and furry tail to pull him out of the hole.
He tugged and yanked until he pulled Koala's tail
right off! Koala's pride and joy was gone forever.

And to this day, all koalas
have short and stumpy tails.
But Koala lost more than his
tail that day. Because he was
lazy and selfish, he also lost
his best friend.

How the kangaroo got her pouch

Back in the Dreamtime, Mother Kangaroo didn't have a pouch to carry her baby. Whenever her back was turned, Joey would hop away to explore, and she was always losing sight of him. She worried that one day he'd hop so far away, she'd lose him forever.

22

On this day, she was cleaning Joey's fur when a weak and skinny old wombat came crawling towards them. Mother Kangaroo had a kind heart and offered to take the hungry creature to where there was water and grass.

With Wombat holding her tail between his teeth, they slowly set off. It wasn't an easy journey. Wombat kept losing his grip, and Joey became tired and grumpy. He wanted his mother to carry him but, like all kangaroos, her arms were too short to hold him properly.

When they reached a grassy water hole, Wombat drank
and ate. Mother Kangaroo watched him, happy that
he was feeling better. She looked around for Joey, but
couldn't see him anywhere. Mother Kangaroo hopped
off to find her baby and was relieved to see him asleep
under a gumtree.

Suddenly, there was a movement in the bushes.
Mother Kangaroo sensed danger. Her nose twitched
and she stood still and straight. It was a hunter
with his eyes fixed on Wombat.
Already his boomerang was raised
above his head, its edges ready
to slice the air.

Mother Kangaroo was scared and wanted to
bound away, but Wombat was as helpless as
a baby; she had to look after him. She bravely
thumped the ground with her feet to make
the hunter turn towards her.
A kangaroo was a much bigger
meal than a wombat so she
knew that, when she bounded
away, he'd chase after her.

And he did. Mother Kangaroo stayed out of the reach
of the hunter's boomerang until he finally gave up, and
then she quietly hopped back to Joey.

Together they looked for Wombat, but he'd vanished!
What they didn't know was that Wombat wasn't actually
a wombat! He was the Sky Father, Byamee, in disguise.
Byamee had come down from the sky world to find
out which creature had the kindest heart. Now he had
his answer.

Byamee wanted to give Mother Kangaroo a gift that would help her. He called the sky spirits together. Byamee told them to go down and peel long strips of bark from a gumtree and make them into an apron. The spirits were to give it to Mother Kangaroo and tell her to tie it around her waist.

The moment Mother Kangaroo tied the apron around her waist, Byamee changed it into a fur and skin pouch. Now she could carry Joey around and he'd never get lost again.

Mother Kangaroo loved her pouch, but she didn't want to be the only mother with one. Her kind heart made her think about others and she wanted her friends to have a pouch, too. Byamee agreed, and the spirits made pouches for all her friends. And that's how the kangaroo got her pouch.

Animal awards

Friendship Award

We award this certificate to

PARROT

Survival Award
We award this certificate to
TREE KANGAROO

Bravery Award
We award this certificate to
MOTHER KANGAROO

Ideas for reading

Written by Clare Dowdall, PhD
Lecturer and Primary Literacy Consultant

Reading objectives:
- identify themes and conventions in a wide range of books
- make predictions from details stated and applied
- identify main ideas drawn from more than one paragraph and summarise ideas

Spoken language objectives:
- give well-structured descriptions, explanations and narratives for different purposes

Curriculum links: Geography – physical geography, Australia; PSHE – health and well-being, achievements

Resources: ICT for research; materials for dot painting

Build a context for reading

- Dreaming stories are passed on by Aboriginal Elders through storytelling (and songs, dances, paintings). These stories are important because they tell us and future generations how Aboriginal people are connected to the land and its living things and the importance of rules, which tell us how to care for each other and the natural environment.
- Ask children to create a list of animals that live in Australia, and think of any special qualities that they have.
- Look at the front cover and ask children to suggest what they think the Australian Dreamtime is.
- Read the blurb. Ask children to explain what Kangaroo pouches are used for and to speculate about how they came to be.

Understand and apply reading strategies

- Read aloud to p4 with the children. Ask them to try to identify each bird in the illustrations, and help them read unfamiliar names.